The Practical Princess
and other
Liberating Fairy Tales

by JAY WILLIAMS

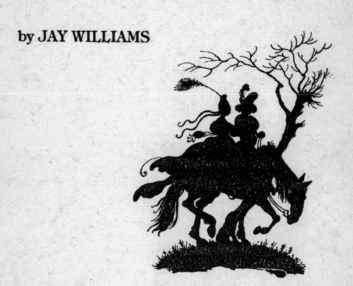

Cover illustration by Marilyn Braaten

Inside illustrations by Rick Schreiter

SCHOLASTIC BOOK SERVICES

NEW YORK • TORONTO • LONDON • AUCKLAND • SYDNEY • TOKYO

ISBN 0-590-31315-0

Text copyright © 1978 by Jay Williams. Illustrations copyright © 1978 by Parents' Magazine Press. All rights reserved. Published by Scholastic Book Services, a division of Scholastic Magazines, Inc.

12 11 10 9 8 7 6 5 4 3 2 1   12   0 1 2 3 4 5/8

CONTENTS

The
Practical Princess
and other
Liberating Fairy Tales

THE PRACTICAL PRINCESS

Princess Bedelia was as lovely as the moon shining upon a lake full of waterlilies. She was as graceful as a cat leaping. And she was also extremely practical.

When she was born, three fairies had come to her cradle to give her gifts as was usual in that country. The first fairy had given her beauty. The second had given her grace. But the third, who was a wise old creature, had said, "I give her common sense."

"I don't think much of that gift," said King Ludwig, raising his eyebrows. "What good is common sense to a princess? All she needs is charm."

Nevertheless, when Bedelia was eighteen years old,

something happened which made the king change his mind.

A dragon moved into the neighborhood. He settled in a dark cave on top of a mountain, and the first thing he did was to send a message to the king. "I must have a princess to devour," the message said, "or I shall breathe out my fiery breath and destroy the kingdom."

Sadly, King Ludwig called together his councilors and read them the message. "Perhaps," said the Prime Minister, "we had better advertise for a knight to slay the dragon? That is what is generally done in these cases."

"I'm afraid we haven't time," answered the king. "The dragon has only given us until tomorrow morning. There is no help for it. We shall have to send him the princess." Princess Bedelia had come to the meeting because, as she said, she liked to mind her own business and this was certainly her business.

"Rubbish!" she said. "Dragons can't tell the difference between princesses and anyone else. Use your common sense. He's just asking for me because he's a snob."

"That may be so," said her father, "but if we don't send you along, he'll destroy the kingdom."

"Right!" said Bedelia. "I see I'll have to deal with this myself." She left the council chamber. She got the largest and gaudiest of her state robes and stuffed it with straw, and tied it together with string. Into the

2

center of the bundle she packed about a hundred pounds of gunpowder. She got two strong young men to carry it up the mountain for her. She stood in front of the dragon's cave, and called, "Come out! Here's the princess!"

The dragon came blinking and peering out of the darkness. Seeing the bright robe covered with gold and silver embroidery, and hearing Bedelia's voice, he opened his mouth wide.

At Bedelia's signal, the two young men swung the robe and gave it a good heave, right down the dragon's throat. Bedelia threw herself flat on the ground, and the two young men ran.

As the gunpowder met the flames inside the dragon, there was a tremendous explosion.

Bedelia got up, dusting herself off. "Dragons," she said, "are not very bright."

She left the two young men sweeping up the pieces, and she went back to the castle to have her geography lesson.

The lesson that morning was local geography. "Our kingdom, Arapathia, is bounded on the north by Istven," said the teacher. "Lord Garp, the ruler of Istven, is old, crafty, rich, and greedy." At that very moment, Lord Garp of Istven was arriving at the castle. Word of Bedelia's destruction of the dragon had reached him. "That girl," said he, "is just the wife for me." And he had come with a hundred finely-dressed courtiers and many presents to ask King Ludwig for her hand.

The king sent for Bedelia. "My dear," he said, clearing his throat nervously, "just see who is here."

"I see. It's Lord Garp," said Bedelia. She turned to go.

"He wants to marry you," said the king.

Bedelia looked at Lord Garp. His face was like an old napkin, crumpled and wrinkled. It was covered with warts, as if someone had left crumbs on the napkin. He had only two teeth. Six long hairs grew from his chin, and none on his head. She felt like screaming.

However, she said, "I'm very flattered. Thank you, Lord Garp. Just let me talk to my father in private for a minute." When they had retired to a small room behind the throne, Bedelia said to the king, "What will Lord Garp do if I refuse to marry him?"

"He is rich, greedy, and crafty," said the king unhappily. "He is also used to having his own way in everything. He will be insulted. He will probably declare war on us, and then there will be trouble."

"Very well," said Bedelia. "We must be practical."

She returned to the throne room. Smiling sweetly at Lord Garp, she said, "My lord, as you know, it is customary for a princess to set tasks for anyone who wishes to marry her. Surely you wouldn't like me to break the custom. And you are bold and powerful enough, I know, to perform any task."

"That is true," said Lord Garp smugly, stroking the six hairs on his chin. "Name your task."

"Bring me," said Bedelia, "a branch from the Jewel Tree of Paxis."

Lord Garp bowed, and off he went. "I think," said Bedelia to her father, "that we have seen the last of him. For Paxis is a thousand miles away, and the Jewel Tree is guarded by lions, serpents, and wolves."

But in two weeks, Lord Garp was back. With him he bore a chest, and from the chest he took a wonderful twig. Its bark was of rough gold. The leaves that grew from it were of fine silver. The twig was covered with blossoms, and each blossom had petals of mother-of-pearl and centers of sapphires, the color of the evening sky.

Bedelia's heart sank as she took the twig. But then she said to herself, "Use your common sense, my girl! Lord Garp never traveled two thousand miles in two

weeks, nor is he the man to fight his way through lions, serpents, and wolves."

She looked carefully at the branch. Then she said, "My lord, you know that the Jewel Tree of Paxis is a living tree, although it is all made of jewels."

"Why, of course," said Lord Garp. "Everyone knows that."

"Well," said Bedelia, "then why is it that these blossoms have no scent?"

Lord Garp turned red.

"I think," Bedelia went on, "that this branch was made by the jewelers of Istven, who are the best in the world. Not very nice of you, my lord. Some people might even call it cheating."

Lord Garp shrugged. He was too old and rich to feel ashamed. But like many men used to having their own way, the more Bedelia refused him, the more he was determined to have her.

"Never mind all that," he said. "Set me another task. This time, I swear I will perform it."

Bedelia sighed. "Very well. Then bring me a cloak made from the skins of the salamanders who live in the Volcano of Scoria."

Lord Garp bowed, and off he went. "The Volcano of Scoria," said Bedelia to her father, "is covered with red-hot lava. It burns steadily with great flames, and pours out poisonous smoke so that no one can come within a mile of it."

"You have certainly profited by your geography lessons," said the king, with admiration.

Nevertheless, in a week, Lord Garp was back. This time, he carried a cloak that shone and rippled like all the colors of fire. It was made of scaly skins, stitched together with golden wire as fine as a hair; and each scale was red and orange and blue, like a tiny flame.

Bedelia took the splendid cloak. She said to herself, "Use your head, miss! Lord Garp never climbed the red-hot slopes of the Volcano of Scoria."

A fire was burning in the fireplace of the throne room. Bedelia hurled the cloak into it. The skins blazed up in a flash, blackened, and fell to ashes.

Lord Garp's mouth fell open. Before he could speak, Bedelia said, "That cloak was a fake, my lord. The skins of salamanders who can live in the Volcano of Scoria wouldn't burn in a little fire like that one."

Lord Garp turned pale with anger. He hopped up and down, unable at first to do anything but splutter.

"Ub—ub—ub!" he cried. Then, controlling himself, he said, "So be it. If I can't have you, no one shall!"

He pointed a long, skinny finger at her. On the finger was a magic ring. At once, a great wind arose. It blew through the throne room. It sent King Ludwig flying one way and his guards the other. It picked up Bedelia and whisked her off through the air. When she

could catch her breath and look about her, she found herself in a room at the top of a tower.

Bedelia peered out of the window. About the tower stretched an empty, barren plain. As she watched, a speck appeared in the distance. A plume of dust rose behind it. It drew nearer and became Lord Garp on horseback.

He rode to the tower and looked up at Bedelia. "Aha!" he croaked. "So you are safe and snug, are you? And will you marry me now?"

"Never," said Bedelia, firmly.

"Then stay there until never comes," snarled Lord Garp.

Away he rode.

For the next two days, Bedelia felt very sorry for herself. She sat wistfully by the window, looking out at the empty plain. When she was hungry, food appeared on the table. When she was tired, she lay down on the narrow cot and slept. Each day, Lord Garp rode by and asked if she had changed her mind, and each day she refused him. Her only hope was that, as so often happens in old tales, a prince might come riding by who would rescue her.

But on the third day, she gave herself a shake.

"Now, then, pull yourself together," she said, sternly. "If you sit waiting for a prince to rescue you, you may sit here forever. Be practical! If there's any rescuing to be done, you're going to have to do it yourself."

She jumped up. There was something she had not yet done, and now she did it. She tried the door.

It opened.

Outside, were three other doors. But there was no sign of a stair, or any way down from the top of the tower.

She opened two of the doors and found that they led into cells just like hers, but empty.

Behind the fourth door, however, lay what appeared to be a haystack.

From beneath it came the sound of snores. And between snores, a voice said, "Sixteen million and twelve...*snore*...sixteen million and thirteen...*snore* ...sixteen million and fourteen...."

Cautiously, she went closer. Then she saw that what she had taken for a haystack was in fact an immense pile of blond hair. Parting it, she found a young man, sound asleep.

As she stared, he opened his eyes. He blinked at her. "Who—?" he said. Then he said, "Sixteen million and fifteen," closed his eyes, and fell asleep again.

Bedelia took him by the shoulder and shook him hard. He awoke, yawning, and tried to sit up. But the mass of hair made this difficult.

"What on earth is the matter with you?" Bedelia asked. "Who are you?"

"I am Prince Perian," he replied, "the rightful ruler of — oh, dear, here I go again. Sixteen million and . . ." His eyes began to close.

Bedelia shook him again. He made a violent effort and managed to wake up enough to continue, " — of Istven. But Lord Garp has put me under a spell. I have to count sheep jumping over a fence, and this puts me to slee — ee — ee —"

He began to snore lightly.

"Dear me," said Bedelia. "I must do something."

She thought hard. Then she pinched Perian's ear, and this woke him with a start. "Listen," she said. "It's quite simple. It's all in your mind, you see. You are imagining the sheep jumping over the fence — No! Don't go to sleep again!

This is what you must do. Imagine them jumping backward. As you do, *count* them backwards and when you get to *one*, you'll be wide awake."

The prince's eyes snapped open. "Marvelous!" he said. "Will it work?"

"It's bound to," said Bedelia. "For if the sheep going one way will put you to sleep, their going back again will wake you up."

Hastily, the prince began to count, "Six million and fourteen, six million and thirteen, six million and twelve . . ."

"Oh, my goodness," cried Bedelia, "count by hundreds, or you'll never get there."

He began to gabble as fast as he could, and with each moment that passed, his eyes sparkled more brightly, his face grew livelier, and he seemed a little stronger, until at last, he shouted, "Five, four, three, two, ONE!" and awoke completely.

He struggled to his feet, with a little help from Bedelia.

"Heavens!" he said. "Look how my hair and beard have grown. I've been here for years. Thank you, my dear. Who are you, and what are you doing here?"

Bedelia quickly explained.

Perian shook his head. "One more crime of Lord Garp's," he said. "We must escape and see that he is punished."

"Easier said than done," Bedelia replied. "There is no stair in this tower, as far as I can tell, and the outside wall is much too smooth to climb."

Perian frowned. "This will take some thought," he said. "What we need is a long rope."

"Use your common sense," said Bedelia. "We haven't any rope."

Then her face brightened, and she clapped her hands. "But we have your beard," she laughed.

Perian understood at once, and chuckled. "I'm sure it will reach almost to the ground," he said. "But we haven't any scissors to cut it off with."

"That is so," said Bedelia. "Hang it out of the window and let me climb down. I'll search the tower and perhaps I can find a ladder, or a hidden stair. If all else fails, I can go for help."

She and the prince gathered up great armfuls of the beard and staggered into Bedelia's room, which had the largest window. The prince's long hair trailed behind and nearly tripped him.

He threw the beard out of the window, and sure enough the end of it came to within a few feet of the ground.

Perian braced himself, holding the beard with both hands to ease the pull on his chin. Bedelia climbed out of the window and slid down the beard. She dropped to the ground and sat for a moment, breathless.

And as she sat there, out of the wilderness came the drumming of hoofs, a cloud of dust, and then Lord Garp on his swift horse.

With one glance, he saw what was happening. He shook his fist up at Prince Perian.

"Meddlesome fool!" he shouted. "I'll teach you to interfere."

He leaped from the horse and grabbed the beard. He gave it a tremendous yank. Headfirst came Perian, out of the window. Down he fell, and with a thump, he landed right on top of old Lord Garp.

This saved Perian, who was not hurt at all. But it was the end of Lord Garp.

Perian and Bedelia rode back to Istven on Lord Garp's horse.

In the great city, the prince was greeted with cheers of joy — once everyone had recognized him after so many years and under so much hair.

And of course, since Bedelia had rescued him from captivity, she married him. First, however, she made him get a haircut and a shave so that she could see what he really looked like.

For she was always practical.

STUPID MARCO

The youngest son of the King of Lirripipe was
called Marco. That is, he was called Marco—or
Your Highness — in public. But among themselves,
people spoke of him as "Poor dear Marco," or "Alas,
poor Marco," or just sighed and rolled their eyes. This
was because, although he was cheerful and good-
hearted and handsome, he was not bright enough to tell
his right hand from his left.

He was not exactly stupid. But then, neither was he
exactly as brilliant as a prince ought to be. His two
older brothers quickly passed all their classes in gov-
ernment, politics, courtly bowing, economics, arith-

metic, and science. But Marco looked out the window and smiled and hummed and made up poetry. It wasn't bad poetry, but on every one of his classroom papers his instructor sadly wrote, *Failed*.

However, Marco had three great accomplishments. In the first place, he was so charming and pleasant a person that no one could help liking him and wanting to help him. Secondly, he could whistle very loudly between his fingers. And thirdly, he knew an infallible cure for hiccups.

In consequence, people found excuses for him. Nobody minded very much his being a little slow-witted, and he was popular everywhere in the kingdom.

One day, his father called Marco into the throne room.

"My dear boy," he said, "the time has come for you to undertake your Quest. As you know, it is the custom in Lirripipe for every young prince, when he has finished his schooling, to go forth and rescue a princess for his bride. Your two older brothers have successfully done so. Now it is your turn."

"Yes, father," said Marco. "My turn for what?"

The king sighed and patiently repeated what he had said. "I am going to make it easy for you," he went on.

"There is a very nice princess named Aurelia, who is being held prisoner in a tower not far from here. I have written instructions for rescuing her on this piece of paper. You will set out tomorrow morning early and go three miles to the south. When you come to the fork in the road, turn left and continue until you come to the tower. Then follow the instructions."

"Certainly, Father," said Marco. "But how will I know which way is left?"

"I have thought of that, too," said the king, taking up the golden pen and inkwell which stood beside his throne.

The following morning, Marco set out. Mounted on his fine black steed with his sword by his side he looked more handsome than ever. And on the backs of his hands were written the words *right* and *left*.

His mother kissed him good-bye and then stood back to wave. "Oh, dear, I hope he can stay out of trouble," she murmured to the king.

"Well, my love," said the king, "he does have certain accomplishments. He is so amiable and attractive that I am sure he will find people to help him wherever he goes. And as a last resort, he can cure someone's hiccups, or whistle."

Off went Marco. For the first mile, he rode merrily enough. Then it began to rain. Down it came, until the feather on his hat was bent, and his clothes were drenched. Of course, he had forgotten his raincoat. He kept up his spirits, however, by singing songs to himself, and at last he came to the fork in the road.

He looked down at his hands. But on the back of each hand there was only a blue smear. The rain had washed away the ink.

"I'll just have to make a guess," said Marco. And he took the road to the right.

He traveled on and on. The rain stopped, the sun came out and warmed and dried him. Mile after mile he traveled, for many days. At last, one day after he had ridden to the top of a hill, he saw spread out below him a glittering city. He rode down to it and entered the gates.

In the center of the city was an elegant castle. In the downstairs window of one of its towers a maiden sat with her chin on her hand, staring in to space. Her smooth brown hair hung in long braids tied with golden bows, and her eyes were the color of forget-me-nots.

Marco took off his hat. "Good morning!" he said. "Are you the Princess Aurelia?"

The girl yawned. "Never heard of her," she said.

Marco shook his head. "Ah, well, I've done it again," said he. "You see, I have to rescue Princess Aurelia. My father said she was in a tower not far from our kingdom, but I've traveled for miles and miles. I must have taken the wrong road. I *thought* it seemed rather a long way. I'm afraid," he finished with an engaging grin, "I'm not very smart. I can't even tell my right hand from my left."

The girl stopped yawning and looked at him more closely. Then she smiled in return. "My dear," she said, "you aren't fit to be out alone. You need someone to look after you. I'd better go along with you and help you find this princess."

"That would be marvelous," said Marco. "But I haven't the faintest idea where she is."

"Well," said the girl, "my father has a magical parrot which can answer any question put to it. If you'll wait a moment, I'll get the bird, and we'll see if we can locate her."

She helped Marco climb in through the window. "My name," she said, "is Sylvia."

Marco introduced himself. Then Sylvia went off and fetched the parrot. It was made all of ivory, with emerald eyes, and it sat on a perch of gold.

Sylvia asked, "Where is the Princess Aurelia?"

The parrot whirred and ticked. Then it said, "She is

shut up in the Green Glass Tower among the hills of Gargovir."

"Ah," said Sylvia. "And how do we get there from here?"

Again, the parrot ticked and whirred. "Only one person can tell you how to reach the Green Glass Tower," it croaked. "A maiden named Roseanne who lives in the village of Dwindle."

"Good," said Sylvia. "I know where Dwindle is, at any rate. We'll leave at once."

They set out together, Sylvia on a milk-white horse. The way was shortened by Marco, who told stories and

sang songs and recited his verses. By the time they got to Dwindle, Sylvia remarked thoughtfully, "I'm not sure it matters all that much, knowing your right hand from your left."

A friendly innkeeper showed them the house where the maiden, Roseanne, lived. "Don't bother knocking," he said "because she never answers. Just go right in — if you can get the door open," he added, rather mysteriously.

They tied up their horses outside the cottage. It was a pretty place, thatched with straw and covered with honeysuckle which perfumed the air. They pushed at the door and after a struggle got it open. Then they saw why it had been so difficult. The floor was covered with gold pieces which had piled up against the door like a drift of yellow snow.

A girl was washing dishes with her back to the door. She was humming and making such a clatter in the sink that she hadn't heard Marco and Sylvia enter.

Marco cleared his throat and said, "I beg your pardon."

The girl turned around. "Oh! You startled me," she exclaimed.

Four bright gold pieces fell from her mouth and clinked to the floor.

The girl clapped her hand to her forehead and said, "Drat!"

Another gold piece dropped from her lips. She took down a large pad that hung on the wall and began writing busily on it. Marco and Sylvia came and looked curiously over her shoulders.

"I am Roseanne. Welcome," the girl wrote. "As you see, I have something of a problem. Some time ago, I saved the life of the good fairy, Melynda. As a reward, she said to me, "My child, since you are poor but kind, a gold piece shall fall from your mouth with every word you speak.'"

"Heavens!" said Sylvia. "Can't you make her change her mind?"

"I don't know how to find her," Roseanne wrote, mournfully. Then she added, as an afterthought, "I'm sorry about the floor. I had some friends in for a party last night, and I haven't had a chance to sweep up yet."

"I do wish I could help you somehow," Marco said, earnestly. "I don't know any magic, but I do know an infallible cure for hiccups. Would you say that what you have is a kind of hiccups?"

"It wouldn't hurt to try," Roseanne said, clasping her hands. Five more gold pieces went jingling down to join the rest.

"Very well," said Marco. "You must put your head in a large paper bag. Hold your breath while I count ten, and then breathe in and out through your mouth ten times."

Roseanne got out a paper bag and did as he ordered. When at last she took it off her head, they gazed at her in suspense. "Speak!" said Sylvia.

"I'm afraid to," Roseanne replied. But nothing happened — not a gold piece appeared. With a look of joy, she touched her lips "It worked!" she said "I'm cured."

She burst into laughter and, throwing her arms around Marco, gave him a kiss.

"What can I do to show my gratitude?" she said.

"You can tell us how to get to the Green Glass Tower," said Marco. "I have to rescue a princess there."

Roseanne nodded. "I can tell you how to get to the Green Glass Tower," she said, "but alas, my telling you won't do you much good. The tower is a hundred and ninety miles from here, beyond deep ravines, high mountains, pits full of flame, the Direful Mud, the Bottomless Bog, and the River of Knives."

"Dear me," said Marco.

"The only way to get there," Roseanne continued, "is to use the seven-league boots belonging to Fylfot the Necromancer, who lives at the other end of this village."

"Do you think he would lend them to me?" Marco asked, worriedly.

"He will lend them to you," Roseanne replied, "if you give him something he needs, which he doesn't know he wants and which he won't know he has when he gets it."

Poor Marco looked at her in bewilderment. "I can't even remember the beginning of that sentence," he said. "What does it mean?"

"I don't know," said Roseanne, "but I know that it is so."

"Never mind," Sylvia put in. "We'll go and see this Necromancer. Perhaps he'll help Marco anyway."

Bidding Roseanne farewell, they went to the other end of the village. A tall, narrow, dark house stood alone in a garden of toadstools. At an open window high under the eaves sat the Necromancer. He had his back to the window and was reading.

"Good afternoon, sir," called Marco.

The Necromancer did not stir.

"Good afternoon," Marco repeated, more loudly. "Hey! *Yoo-hoo!* SIR!

"He must be deaf as a post," remarked Sylvia.

Now in fact, the Necromancer was not usually deaf. But some days before, while engaged in magic, he had dropped a heavy spell on the foot of a small but bad-tempered imp. In revenge, the imp had settled invisibly on the Necromancer's head and plugged up his ears with its fingers.

Sylvia said to Marco, "Give him a whistle, and maybe that will attract his attention."

Marco put his fingers between his lips and whistled. It was so loud and shrill a whistle that chimneys in the village shook. Birds fell out of the sky covering their ears with their wings. And the invisible imp with a squeak of fright left the Necromancer's head and flew off into the next kingdom.

The Necromancer, of course, did not know what had happened. He had not heard Marco's whistle, nor had he known that the imp was plugging up his ears.

All he knew was that suddenly he could hear again. The clock was ticking. The wind was rustling the leaves. He turned and glanced out of the window and saw a handsome young man and a pretty girl standing in the street staring up at him.

"Good afternoon," he said. "Were you waiting to see me?"

"We need your help," Marco answered, "but I hope we haven't disturbed you."

"Disturbed me? Certainly not," said the Necromancer. He found that he was suddenly feeling very fit and he thought to himself that this fine young man deserved his attention.

He hurried downstairs and let Marco and Sylvia in. "What can I do for you?" he said.

"Please lend me your seven-league boots," said Marco. "I have to go to the Green Glass Tower to rescue Princess Aurelia."

The Necromancer looked grave. "My friend," he said, "I will lend you the boots with pleasure. But I am sorry to say that if you go to that tower you will be going to your death. For there is a two-headed giant on guard, and he is under orders to slay any young man who comes to the gate."

"I shall just have to take a chance," said Marco. "Please let me have the boots."

The Necromancer got them out of a closet and blew the dust off them. "I don't travel much at my age," he explained. "Now, there is one small difficulty. With each step you take in these boots, you will go seven leagues.

Since a league is three miles, seven leagues is twenty-one miles. However, the Green Glass Tower is exactly one hundred and ninety miles away, and twenty-one does not go into a hundred and ninety. If you can wait a little while, I will figure out for you how you can go a hundred and ninety miles in strides of twenty-one miles each."

"How long will it take you?" demanded Sylvia.

"About three days, I should think" said the Necromancer.

"Never mind," Sylvia said, briskly. "I know what to do. Put on the boots, Marco."

Marco slipped them on over his own boots, like galoshes. "What now?" he said.

26

"Now, you may take nine giant strides," Sylvia replied.

He seized her around the waist and off he went. With every stride they sailed high in the air. Far below, they could see jagged cliffs, deep holes darting out fire, a smoking sea of mud, a black quaking bog, and the glitter of a river of sharp steel blades. But with each stride, Marco managed to touch clear ground and then he was off again, soaring over all the obstacles.

With the ninth stride, they stood in safety among grassy hills. Marco looked about. "I don't see any tower," he said.

"We have come 189 miles," said Sylvia. "We shall have to walk the last mile."

Marco slipped off the boots and tucked them under his arm. He and Sylvia began walking, and to pass the time, Marco sang songs and told jokes.

Before long, they saw rising up before them a shining round tower of dark green glass, as smooth and as cold as ice.

They stopped a short distance away and stared at it. No one could possibly climb the walls. There were no windows, for of course in a glass tower one wouldn't need any. Before the front gate stood a giant with two heads. Both his faces were hideous and frowning. He bore a club twice as long as a man, bristling with iron spikes.

27

Suddenly Marco snapped his fingers. "My father gave me instructions for rescuing the princess," he said. "I have them right here." He looked in his wallet. He searched through his pockets. "No I haven't," he said, glumly. "I must have lost them on the road, in the rainstorm."

"Oh, Marco!" said Sylvia. And she almost added, "What an idiot!" But she liked him far too much for that, so instead she said, "I have an idea. Wait right here, and don't move."

"All right," said Marco. Then he said, "Wait for what? What are you going to do?"

"I'm going into the tower," said Sylvia, calmly.

"But — "

"Don't worry. The monster has instructions to bash any young man who comes to the gate. But I'm a girl."

She marched to the gateway. Sure enough, although the giant glared at her with all four of his eyes, he didn't move. Sylvia entered the tower.

In the great hall, she found an old man mopping the floor.

"Is there a princess named Aurelia here?" she asked.

The caretaker leaned on his mop and eyed her. "Why, my dearie," he cackled, "if you've come to visit her, you're just too late. She was rescued yesterday by as nice a young man as ever I did see."

"What?" cried Sylvia. "How did he manage?"

"Had a bit of paper, he had, that told him what to do," said the caretaker. "He said he found it by the roadside. He came in by the back door, you see. No giants there."

"Bother," said Sylvia. "Thank you very much."

She went back to join Marco, and broke the news to him.

"What a shame," said Marco, looking very downcast. "Of course, I don't mean it's a shame about Aurelia; I'm glad she was rescued. But I just can't seem to do anything right. What on earth am I going to say to the king, my father?"

"I suppose," said Sylvia, thoughtfully, "no other princess will do? It *had* to be Aurelia?"

Marco brightened. "Why, no. All I have to do is rescue a princess," he said. "Any princess — it doesn't really matter which one."

"In that case, everything is all right," said Sylvia. "I am a princess."

"You are? How splendid?" Marco said. "What shall I rescue you from?"

"You've already rescued me," Sylvia answered. "You rescued me from boredom. Until you came along, I was ready to scream with weariness and dullness. But with you, I've never known a dull moment."

Marco laughed with delight and took her in his arms. Then his face fell again. "No, it won't do," he said. "Why, I can't even tell my right hand from my left."

"That doesn't matter in the slightest," said Sylvia. "You'll have me, and I can always tell you which is which."

They kissed each other and turned about, and set out hand in hand for home.

THE SILVER WHISTLE

The Wise Woman of the West had a daughter whose name was Prudence. She was a cheerful girl, as wise as her name, and as plain as the day is long.

She had a snub nose, a wide mouth, straight straw-colored hair, and so many freckles that it looked as if someone had sprinkled her with cinnamon.

When the time came for the Wise Woman of the West to die, she called her daughter to her and said, "My dear, you must go out and make your way in the world. I can do nothing about your looks, but you have a merry heart and a lively mind, and there are plenty of people who like freckles. All that I have to give you is this silver whistle. If you blow it once, the birds will come to your call. If you blow it twice, the insects will be your friends. If you blow it three times the beasts will speak to you. Thus you will never be lonely."

"Suppose I were to blow it four times?" asked Prudence. "Try not to do so," said her mother, gravely. "For if you do, it will make a sound shrill enough to shatter glass, and the whistle will be broken."

So off Prudence went to make her way in the world, with nothing but the clothes on her back and the silver whistle in her pocket. She traveled for many a day and many a mile, and at last she came to a house that stood on four legs, in the middle of a wood. The house turned round to face her, and out came an old witch. She was as dry as a winter leaf, and had only a few brown teeth.

"What do you want?" said she.

"I am making my way in the world," said Prudence. "Have you any work for me?"

"Plenty of work," cackled the witch. "And a silver penny on the first day of every month if you do whatever I ask."

"I don't mind," said Prudence. "It will make a nice change."

She became the witch's servant, and if the work was hard it was also interesting, for the witch did magic from morning to night, and there were always plenty of visitors. Whenever Prudence was lonely, she blew her silver whistle and talked to a bird, a bee, or a beast.

One day, a messenger from the king came through the forest. He had a proclamation which he had been commanded to read in every corner of the kingdom. It said:

On the thirty-first day of May, Prince Pertinel is to be married. Therefore, all the maidens of the land are to come to the palace so that the prince may choose the one who suits him best, to be his bride.

Signed, King Quither V.

"Very good," said the witch. "I have a mind to be chosen. For there is nothing I'd like better than to be a princess, and someday queen."

"Dear me," said Prudence, and she couldn't help chuckling. "It seems to me that you would have even less of a chance than I, for if I am plain you are perfectly hideous."

"So you think," retorted the witch. "But with the magical mirror of Morna I will win the prince's heart. For whoever looks into that mirror becomes more beautiful than the dawn of a spring morning. The spell lasts as long as the mirror lasts, and that will be long enough for me."

"And have you the mirror of Morna?" asked Prudence.

"No," said the witch. "But you are going to get it for me."

"I am? Where is it, and how shall I get it?"

"It is kept in the treasure house of The Wazar," the witch said. "And I don't know how you are going to get it. But however you get it, it must be given to you freely or its magic will not work."

"That doesn't make things any easier," murmured Prudence. "Where is the treasure house of The Wazar?"

"I don't know that either," said the witch. "All I know is that it is far to the south, in a land where the trees have leaves but no branches and where the ground moves when the wind blows."

"I have never heard of such a place," Prudence said.

"Well, are you going?"

"I don't mind," said Prudence. "It will make a nice change."

She packed a loaf of bread and a piece of cheese in her handkerchief and put her silver whistle in her pocket. Then she said to the witch, "By the way, what exactly is a Wazar?"

"Nobody knows," said the witch. "I wish you luck."

Off went Prudence, traveling south under the great trees of the forest. She wandered for many days. She was chilled by the wind and made wet by the rain. Sometimes she rested at inns or in the cottages of farmers. Sometimes she ate nothing but dry bread for her dinner and slept on the hard ground. Whenever she felt lonely, she blew her whistle and talked to a bird, a bee, or a beast. She remained as cheerful as she could, and journeyed on, looking for a land where the trees had leaves but no branches and where the ground moved when the wind blew.

After a time, she climbed a steep mountain and came down its other side onto a wide plain. The sun blazed overhead. There were tall trees with rough, scaly trunks and from their tops grew large graceful leaves like bunches of feathers. Underfoot, the ground was soft sand, and when the wind blew, the sand stirred and shifted.

"Ah," said Prudence. "This must be the land of The Wazar."

Not far away was a magnificent palace built of white marble. There were a thousand windows in its high walls. From a hundred spires and domes flew banners of red and gold. Prudence walked to the palace and stood before the gates.

They were wide open.

"I suppose that means I can go in," she said.

She entered and found herself in a large hall. It was splendidly furnished but everything was covered with dust. Spiderwebs hung from the ceiling. No servant came forward, and no guard stopped her. All was empty, silent, and dirty.

She passed through it into a corridor. She found a number of fine rooms, and all were as empty and as untended as the first. In the last room, seated on a chair studded with diamonds was a fat moon-faced man. He wore a tall red hat with a diamond on the front of it. His robes were embroidered with golden threads. Although the chair didn't look very comfortable, he was sound asleep with his hands clasped on his round stomach.

Prudence cleared her throat. "Good day," she said.

He opened one eye and then the other.

"I am looking for The Wazar," she said.

"Then you can stop looking and go away," said the man, closing his eyes again.

"Why do they call you *The* Wazar?" asked Prudence.

His eyes snapped open and he sat up. "Because I am the only one there is," he answered. "Why do you want to know?"

"I'm curious. What is a Wazar?"

"I am, of course. And now that we're asking questions, who are you and what are you doing here?"

Prudence decided it might be better to say nothing about the mirror until she found out a bit more about The Wazar.

"My name is Prudence, and I'm making my way through the world," said she.

The Wazar stroked his ginger-colored whiskers. "Hm," he said. "I don't suppose you're looking for a job, are you? All my servants have run off and left me."

"I don't mind," said Prudence. "It will make a nice change. Why did your servants leave you?"

"It is surprising, isn't it?" said The Wazar. "I am one of the kindest, most generous men imaginable. I suppose they were frightened because my neighbor,

Arbroag the Unpleasant, has threatened to destroy me."

"Why should he do that?"

"Well," said The Wazar, "we Wazars, as you may know, are fond of diamonds. And since I am the only Wazar there is, I am even fonder of them than anyone. I stole a tiny little diamond from Arbroag — it only weighed about forty pounds—and when he demanded it back, I told him in the quietest and friendliest way that he was a thick-headed pig-snouted ring-tailed guttersnipe. For some reason he became angry and put a curse on me."

"I see," said Prudence. "When does he plan to destroy you?"

"Tonight," said The Wazar, gloomily. "And I haven't even had my dinner."

"Goodness!" said Prudence. "It doesn't sound as though a job with you would last very long."

"If you will work for me until sunrise tomorrow," said The Wazar, "and help me to escape from Arbroag's curse, I will give you whatever you wish from my treasure house. However," he added, quickly, "you must let *me* choose what it shall be."

Prudence laughed. "Very well," she said. "What do you want me to do first?"

"First of all," said The Wazar, folding his hands over his stomach again, "clean up the palace. It's a mess."

Prudence looked about for a broom.

"Oh, I forgot to mention," said The Wazar, "that part of the curse Arbroag put on me was that here no broom will sweep and no mop will mop. Now, you'd better get busy."

For a moment, Prudence stood, just thinking. Then she took out her silver whistle and blew a blast on it.

In a twinkling, the air was full of birds. Hundreds and thousands of them came, flapping and chirping.

Their wings blew away the dust. The larger birds picked up the bigger bits of rubbish; the smaller ones took grains of dirt or spiderwebs. Then they flew off, and when they had gone the palace was clean.

The Wazar pointed to one feather which remained on the floor. "Not very neat," he said. "And the noise of the birds has given me a headache. Now I'd like some dinner."

He led Prudence to the kitchen. But before she could begin to cook, it grew dark. It was not the darkness of night, but a deeper darkness as if every light everywhere in the world had been blown out. The Wazar's teeth could be heard chattering.

"I can't bear this," he groaned. "Do something!"

Prudence tried to light a candle. But although it flamed up, it gave off only a tiny glow, like the faint glimmer of a distant star.

"I forgot to tell you," said The Wazar, "that part of the curse Arbrog put on me was that when the darkness comes no lamp nor candle will give light."

Prudence took out her silver whistle and blew two blasts on it. At once, millions of fireflies came from the desert. They swarmed in at the windows and hung in clusters in the air. All their shining bodies together were like bright moonlight.

Prudence soon had a fire going in the stove and was able to cook a fine stew. The Wazar wrapped his robe about him, sat down at the kitchen table and ate with a hearty appetite.

"It's not exactly what I'm used to," he complained. "I would have preferred roast pheasant, sugared rose petals, and champagne. However, I suppose this is the best you can do."

Prudence thought she could understand why all his servants had left him. She said nothing, however, but helped herself to some stew.

Then it began to grow cold. Frost formed on the windows and walls. Icicles hung glittering from the rafters. And the flames of the fire in the stove froze and stood fixed as if they were made of yellow glass.

"I forgot to tell you," whispered The Wazar, "that part of the curse Abroag put on me was that when the cold comes no flame nor fire will warm me. This is the end. Good-bye."

"Nonsense!" said Prudence. "You hired me to save you and that's what I intend to do."

She took out her silver whistle and blew three blasts on it.

In the door bounded a lion.

The lion uttered a roar, and out by the other door bounded The Wazar. The lion ran after him. All through the palace they went, in one room and out the other, up stairs and down, and every time The Wazar stopped to catch his breath the lion would snarl and chase him again.

He grew hot from running. Sweat dripped down his

face and stained his robe, and his cheeks were redder than his hat.

When at last the sun rose, he was thinner than he had been but warm and still alive.

"Now," said Prudence, "it is sunrise and I have done as you asked."

"That's true," said The Wazar, peevishly, "but I have lost ten pounds and I've had no sleep. However, I forgive you, for as I told you I am a kind and generous man. Come along with me to my treasure house."

The treasure house was heaped high with The Wazar's collection of diamonds. Diamonds of all shapes, colors, and sizes lay there in dazzling heaps. Prudence looked thoughtfully at a very fine green diamond which was about the size of a St. Bernard dog.

The Wazar turned pale. Before he could speak, Prudence said, "You were quite right when you said that you wanted to choose what I should take. All these

diamonds are too big and too heavy. Pick something
that will do for a girl like me."

The Wazar sighed with relief. Climbing a ladder to
the topmost shelf, he took down a plain, simple mirror
of ivory.

"This is the magical mirror of Morna," he said,
blowing the dust off it. "It is said to make people
beautiful. It's no use to me, as I'm already as beautiful
as possible. But it might do you some good."

"You are right," said Prudence. "Do you give it to me
freely?"

"Absolutely," said The Wazar, and he pushed her
out the door and locked it behind him with sixteen
keys.

Prudence started for home. When she had gone a mile or two, she thought, perhaps I might just take a peep into the mirror and see if it makes me beautiful. She was beginning to unwrap it, and then she laughed.

"I don't think I want to be beautiful," she said. "I might be different outside but I'd be the same inside, and I'm used to me the way I am. Anyway, I don't own the mirror, for I only got it for the witch." So she wrapped it up again and went on her way, as cheerfully as ever.

When she came, at last, to the witch's house, it was the thirty-first of May. The witch came out screeching with impatience, and even the house hopped from foot to foot.

"High time you returned, you lazy thing!" she screamed. "Bring the mirror and follow me. We must hurry to the king's palace."

The city was full of girls. Smiling, they went in through the front door of the palace. Sadly, they filed out through the back door.

When Prudence and the witch arrived, there were only a few girls waiting to enter, for it was nearly evening. At the door of the palace, the witch held out her hand. Prudence gave her the mirror.

The witch gazed into it. Instantly, she straightened and grew taller. Her white hair turned to gold. Her face changed and she became so beautiful that all the birds began to sing as if it were the dawn of a spring morning.

Into the palace she went, with Prudence behind her. There sat the king and queen, and before them stood Prince Pertinel. He was a tall, handsome young man, but pale with weariness, and his eyes were glazed from the sight of so many maidens.

Prudence looked at the prince and then she looked at the witch. Although the witch's face was lovely, her eyes had not changed. They were old and hard, and full of witchcraft. She was different outside but the same inside.

"He must not marry her," Prudence said to herself. "If someday she becomes queen, she will be full of wickedness."

There was no help for it. With a sigh, Prudence took out her silver whistle and blew four blasts on it.

With the last note, the whistle split in two. But the mirror cracked with a loud noise and shattered to bits. And as the pieces clattered to the floor, the witch changed again into her own shape. With a screech of rage, she flew straight up into the air and vanished through the ceiling, leaving a large and untidy hole in the plaster.

Prince Pertinel stepped forward and took Prudence by the hand.

"Marvelous!" he said. "You are the girl for me."

Prudence stared at him in surprise.

"Me? But I'm not beautiful," she said.

The prince smiled. "That is true," he said. "But I never said I would choose the most beautiful girl in the kingdom. I only said I would choose the one who suited me best. As it happens, I prefer freckles. Will you marry me?"

"Oh, well, I don't mind," said Prudence, returning his smile. "It will make a nice change."

FORGETFUL FRED

The richest man in the land, even richer than the king, was Bumberdumble Pott. He lived in an enormous house with forty-four rooms, and he had nine cooks, twelve housemaids, four butlers, sixteen helpers, and a young man named Fred who did everything that was left over.

Fred was good-looking and bright, but he was very absent-minded. This was because his head was full of music. When he should have been thinking about his job, he was thinking of songs instead, and when he should have been working, he was playing on his flute. If Bumberdumble Pott said to him, "Fred, throw out the rubbish and hang up my coat," Fred was just as apt to throw away the coat and hang up the rubbish.

In spite of this, Bumberdumble liked him and so did everyone else, because he was merry, kind, friendly, and always polite.

One day, Bumberdumble called together all the servants in the great hall of his house. Standing on the staircase where everyone could see and hear him, he said, "As you all know, I am the richest man in the land."

Everyone nodded. They knew.

"You might think I'd be very happy," Bumberdumble continued, "but I'm not. There is one thing I've wanted all my life, and that is the Bitter Fruit of Satisfaction. When I was young, I could have gone to find it but I was too busy making money. Now I am too old to make the journey. But if one of you will go and get it for me, I will give him half my wealth so that he will be as rich as I am."

Everyone thought that over. At last, the youngest of the butlers said, "Where is the Bitter Fruit of Satisfaction?"

Bumberdumble looked worried. "I am afraid it is a long way off," he admitted. "It is beyond six mountains and six sandy deserts, beyond the Boiling River and the Grimly Wood. And it is guarded by a Fire Drake."

"A Fire Drake? What's that? Something like a dragon?"

"Worse than a dragon," said Bumberdumble gloomily. "Much worse."

"Well," said the youngest of the butlers, "I can't go. I have to finish my job polishing the silver."

"I can't go," said the chief cook. "I have a wife and four children."

"I certainly can't go," said the oldest housemaid. "I have a sore knee."

And the more the others thought about the distance and the difficulties and the Fire Drake at the end of it, the more they thought of reasons why they couldn't go.

But finally, Fred said, "I'll go."

"You?" everyone cried.

"Why not?" said Fred, cheerfully. "I haven't any wives or children, I'm healthy, and you can always hire someone else to take over my jobs."

"But you'll forget where you're going before you've gone a mile," said the chief butler, with a chuckle.

"I will give him a map," said Bumberdumble. He came down the stairs and clapped Fred on the shoulder. "Bring me back the Bitter Fruit, my boy, and you will be richer than a king."

The next morning Fred set out. He had a knapsack full of food on his back, his flute in his pocket, a staff to lean on, and twenty gold pieces in his purse. He also had a map showing where the Bitter Fruit was, and Bumberdumble had hung this around his neck so he wouldn't forget to look at it.

Fred traveled for a whole, long year. He climbed six high and rocky mountains, almost freezing at the tops of them. He tramped across six sandy deserts, almost dying of thirst. He crossed the Boiling River by going to its narrowest place and jumping from one slippery stone to another.

And one evening, he came to an old dark house that stood on the edge of a vast dark wood. He was very weary, hungry, and tattered. His money had long ago been spent. He felt as if he could go no farther.

He knocked at the door, and it was opened by a pretty girl with blue eyes, black hair, and a smudge of dirt on her nose.

"Good evening," said Fred, politely, and then he dropped his staff and would have fallen, but the girl caught his arm and helped him into the house.

There was a bright fire burning and a good smell of cooking in the air.

The girl sat Fred down at the long table and put a bowl of soup in front of him. While he ate, she sat down opposite and watched him.

"You've come a long way," she said.

Fred told her who he was and where he was going. "And I have no idea how to take the Bitter Fruit when I find it," he said sadly, "or how I shall escape the Fire Drake. But if you will let me stay here until I'm rested, maybe I will think of something."

"This isn't my house," said the girl. "It belongs to the Witch of Grimly Wood. She's at a witchery meeting now, and while she's away you may certainly rest here and get your strength back. But when she returns, I don't know whether she'll let you stay, for she is the stingiest person in the world. Perhaps you can pay her in some way?"

"All I have is some music," said Fred. "What's your name?"

"Melissa," said the girl.

"Then I'll play you some special Melissa music, by way of thanks," said Fred.

He put the flute to his lips. His music was like the clear calling of summer birds at evening. Melissa listened and sighed. That night, Fred slept on the floor in front of the fire. The next day he rested and played his flute and told stories about his travels and made Melissa laugh. Working for a witch, she didn't get the chance to laugh very often. She was a good cook and fed him well, and she thought she had never liked anyone half so much.

The following morning, she said, "I am going to help you. I have three gifts my father gave me before he died, and I'll lend them to you. Maybe they will help you get the Bitter Fruit."

She brought out a pair of red slippers, a hat with a feather in it, and a sword.

"These," she said, "are the Shoes of Swiftness, the Cap of Darkness, and the Sword of Sharpness. The shoes will make you run swifter than an arrow, the cap will make you invisible, and the sword will cut through anything."

"Fine!" said Fred. "If I'm invisible, maybe I can steal the Bitter Fruit. If not, maybe I can kill the Fire Drake with the sword. And if that fails, I can run like anything."

At that moment they heard a noise outside.

"It's the witch," said Melissa. "Don't say a word to her about where you're going or how much Bumberdumble is going to pay you. She loves gold more than anything."

The door swung open. In came a puff of cold gray air, and with it the witch.

"Aha!" she croaked. "A stranger! Who are you, and what do you mean by sitting in my kitchen and eating my food?"

"My name is Fred," said Fred. And then, being absent-minded, he promptly forgot about Melissa's warning. "I'm on my way to get the Bitter Fruit of Satisfaction," he said. "When I take it back to Bumberdumble Pott, he will give me half his gold and I'll be richer than a king."

"Is that so?" said the witch. "I know where the Bitter Fruit is — it's just the other side of the Grimly Wood. I'll get it and give it to Bumberdumble Pott and collect the gold myself!" She spun around on her toe, jumped on her broomstick, and shot out of the room, slamming the door behind her.

"Quick!" cried Melissa. "The shoes!"

Fred pulled on the red slippers. He leaped up and off he ran. But not very far.

He had forgotten to open the door. *Thump!* He ran headfirst into it and knocked himself flat.

He struggled up, rubbing his head. "I told you I was absent-minded, didn't I?" he said.

"Never mind," said Melissa. "I'll show you a short cut. With the magic shoes, you can still get there first."

She led him outside and showed him a secret path among the trees. "This will take you straight through Grimly Wood," said she, "to a high hedge of thorns. On the other side of the hedge is the Bitter Fruit."

The Shoes of Swiftness carried Fred along the path like a flash of light from the eye of a lighthouse. At the high thorny hedge he drew the Sword of Sharpness. One-two, he slashed, and made a hole large enough to get through.

On the other side, there was a glass table.

On the table stood a silver tree with one small, dry, brown fruit hanging from it. And behind the table was the Fire Drake. It was scaly and slithery, bigger than a dragon and twice as fierce.

Fred snatched out the Cap of Darkness and put it on his head. But he was so busy looking at the Fire Drake that he wasn't thinking about what he was doing, and he put it on backwards. At once, everything disappeared. Everything but Fred. He couldn't see the Fire Drake or the glass table or the tree. He couldn't even see the ground. It looked as if he were standing on nothing in the middle of nothing.

But he could still feel the earth under his feet. In a panic, he dropped to his hands and knees.

It was the best thing he could have done, for at the same instant the Fire Drake blew out a sheet of flame. It would have crisped Fred up like a piece of burnt toast if it had touched him, but it went right over him.

"Oh," he groaned. "If only I weren't so absent-minded."

He reached up and turned the Cap of Darkness around on his head. Now he could see everything again, but *he* was invisible. He got shakily to his feet. He could see the Fire Drake looking this way and that in puzzlement. He tiptoed over to the silver tree.

The fruit was gone.

He understood what had happened. While the Fire Drake had been shooting its flames at him, the witch had sneaked up and stolen the fruit.

Fred ran back through the Grimly Wood to the witch's house. There was the witch, just packing her suitcase for the long broomstick flight to Bumberdumble's house.

"Stop!" yelled Fred.

With one chop of the Sword of Sharpness he cut her broomstick in two.

The witch snatched a handful of ashes from the fire and threw them into the air. They settled over Fred and then she could see him, like a faint gray shadow.

"So it's you, miserable wretch!" she screamed. "I'll turn you into a piece of waste paper and throw you away."

She began to mumble a wicked spell.

"Stop her!" cried Melissa. "Use your sword!"

Fred lifted the sword. Then he lowered it again. "I can't," he said. "It wouldn't be polite."

The witch raised her hands. The spell was ready.

"Then cut the ground out from under her," snapped Melissa.

Fred whirled the sword. He sliced away the floor under the witch's feet. Down she fell.

Under the floor there was a bottomless well. The witch fell into it and that was the end of her.

Fred removed the Cap of Darkness and dusted himself off. He handed the cap, the shoes, and the sword to Melissa.

"Thank you," he said. "But do you know, I forgot something."

"What?"

"The Bitter Fruit of Satisfaction. I forgot that the witch was holding it. She is still holding it, wherever she is."

"What a shame," said Melissa.

Fred scratched his head.

"Oh, I don't know," he said. "If you will marry me, I would really rather have you than be richer than a king."

So they settled down in the witch's house — after fixing the hole in the floor — and they were happy together. And since Fred could play as much music as he liked whenever he liked, he was never absent-minded again except once in a while.

As for Bumberdumble Pott, if he never got the Bitter Fruit, at any rate he remained the richest man in the land, and that was better than nothing.

PETRONELLA

In the kingdom of Skyclear Mountain, three princes were always born to the king and queen. The oldest prince was always called Michael, the middle prince was always called George, and the youngest was always called Peter. When they were grown, they always went out to seek their fortunes. What happened to the oldest prince and the middle prince no one ever knew. But the youngest prince always rescued a princess, brought her home, and in time ruled over the kingdom. That was the way it had always been. And so far as anyone knew, that was the way it would always be.

Until now.

Now was the time of King Peter the twenty-sixth and Queen Blossom. An oldest prince was born, and a middle prince. But the youngest prince turned out to be a girl.

"Well," said the king gloomily, "we can't call her Peter. We'll have to call her Petronella. And what's to be done about it, I'm sure I don't know."

There was nothing to be done. The years passed, and the time came for the princes to go out and seek their fortunes. Michael and George said good-bye to the king and queen and mounted their horses. Then out came Petronella. She was dressed in traveling clothes, with her bag packed and a sword by her side.

"If you think," she said, "that I'm going to sit at home, you are mistaken. I'm going to seek my fortune, too."

"Impossible!" said the king.

"What will people say?" cried the queen.

"Look," said Prince Michael, "be reasonable, Pet. Stay home. Sooner or later a prince will turn up here."

Petronella smiled. She was a tall, handsome girl with flaming red hair and when she smiled in that particular way it meant she was trying to keep her temper.

"I'm going with you," she said. "I'll find a prince if I have to rescue one from something myself. And that's that."

The grooms brought out her horse, she said good-bye to her parents, and away she went behind her two brothers.

They traveled into the flatlands below Skyclear Mountain. After many days, they entered a great dark forest. They came to a place where the road divided into three, and there at the fork sat a little, wrinkled old man covered with dust and spiderwebs.

Prince Michael said haughtily, "Where do these roads go, old man?"

"The road on the right goes to the city of Gratz," the man replied. "The road in the center goes to the castle of Blitz. The road on the left goes to the house of Albion the enchanter. And that's one."

"What do you mean by 'And that's one'?" asked Prince George.

"I mean," said the old man, "that I am forced to sit on this spot without stirring, and that I must answer one question from each person who passes by. And that's two."

Petronella's kind heart was touched. "Is there anything I can do to help you?" she asked.

The old man sprang to his feet. The dust fell from him in clouds.

"You have already done so," he said. "For that question is the one which releases me. I have sat here for sixty-two years waiting for someone to ask me that." He snapped his fingers with joy. "In return, I will tell you anything you wish to know."

"Where can I find a prince?" Petronella said promptly.

"There is one in the house of Albion the enchanter," the old man answered.

"Ah," said Petronella, "then that is where I am going."

"In that case I will leave you," said her oldest brother. "For I am going to the castle of Blitz to see if I can find my fortune there."

"Good luck," said Prince George. "For I am going to the city of Gratz. I have a feeling my fortune is there."

They embraced her and rode away.

Petronella looked thoughtfully at the old man, who was combing spiderwebs and dust out of his beard. "May I ask you something else?" she said.

"Of course. Anything."

"Suppose I wanted to rescue that prince from the enchanter. How would I go about it? I haven't any experience in such things, you see."

The old man chewed a piece of his beard. "I do not know everything," he said, after a moment. "I know that there are three magical secrets which, if you can get them from him, will help you."

"How can I get them?" asked Petronella.

"Offer to work for him. He will set you three tasks, and if you can do them you may demand a reward for each. You must ask him for a comb for your hair, a mirror to look into, and a ring for your finger."

"And then?"

"I do not know. I only know that when you rescue the prince, you can use these things to escape from the enchanter."

"It doesn't sound easy," sighed Petronella.

"Nothing we really want is easy," said the old man. "Look at me — I have wanted my freedom, and I've had to wait sixty-two years for it."

Petronella said good-bye to him. She mounted her horse and galloped along the third road.

It ended at a low, rambling house with a red roof. It

was a comfortable-looking house, surrounded by gardens and stables and trees heavy with fruit.

On the lawn, in an armchair, sat a handsome young man with his eyes closed and his face turned to the sky.

Petronella tied her horse to the gate and walked across the lawn.

"Is this the house of Albion the enchanter?" she said.

The young man blinked up at her in surprise.

"I think so," he said. "Yes, I'm sure it is."

"And who are you?"

The young man yawned and stretched. "I am Prince Ferdinand of Firebright," he replied. "Would you mind stepping aside? I'm trying to get a suntan and you're standing in the way."

Petronella snorted. "You don't sound like much of a prince," she said.

"That's funny," said the young man, closing his eyes. "That's what my father always says."

At that moment the door of the house opened. Out came a man dressed all in black and silver. He was tall and thin, and his eyes were as black as a cloud full of thunder. Petronella knew at once that he must be the enchanter.

He bowed to her politely. "What can I do for you?"

"I wish to work for you," said Petronella boldly.

Albion nodded. "I cannot refuse you," he said. "But

I warn you, it will be dangerous. Tonight I will give you a task. If you do it, I will reward you. If you fail, you must die."

Petronella glanced at the prince and sighed. "If I must, I must," she said. "Very well."

That evening they all had dinner together in the enchanter's cozy kitchen. Then Albion took Petronella out to a stone building and unbolted its door. Inside were seven huge black dogs.

"You must watch my hounds all night," said he.

Petronella went in, and Albion closed and locked the door.

At once the hounds began to snarl and bark. They bared their teeth at her. But Petronella was a real princess. She plucked up her courage. Instead of backing away, she went toward the dogs. She began to speak to them in a quiet voice. They stopped snarling and sniffed at her. She patted their heads.

"I see what it is," she said. "You are lonely here. I will keep you company."

And so all night long, she sat on the floor and talked to the hounds and stroked them. They lay close to her, panting.

In the morning Albion came and let her out. "Ah," said he, "I see that you are brave. If you had run from the dogs, they would have torn you to pieces. Now you may ask for what you want."

"I want a comb for my hair," said Petronella.

The enchanter gave her a comb carved from a piece of black wood.

Prince Ferdinand was sunning himself and working at a crossword puzzle. Petronella said to him in a low voice, "I am doing this for you."

"That's nice," said the prince. "What's 'selfish' in nine letters?"

"You are," snapped Petronella. She went to the enchanter. "I will work for you once more," she said.

That night Albion led her to a stable. Inside were seven huge horses.

"Tonight," he said, "you must watch my steeds."

He went out and locked the door. At once the horses began to rear and neigh. They pawed at her with their iron hoofs.

But Petronella was a real princess. She looked closely at them and saw that their coats were rough and their manes and tails full of burrs.

"I see what it is," she said. "You are hungry and dirty."

She brought them as much hay as they could eat, and began to brush them. All night long she fed them and groomed them, and they stood quietly in their stalls.

In the morning Albion let her out. "You are as kind as you are brave," said he. "If you had run from them they would have trampled you under their hoofs. What will you have as a reward?"

"I want a mirror to look into," said Petronella.

The enchanter gave her a mirror made of silver.

She looked across the lawn at Prince Ferdinand. He was doing exercises leisurely. He was certainly handsome. She said to the enchanter, "I will work for you once more."

That night Albion led her to a loft above the stables. There, on perches, were seven great hawks.

"Tonight," said he, "you must watch my falcons."

As soon as Petronella was locked in, the hawks began to beat their wings and scream at her.

Petronella laughed. "That is not how birds sing," she said. "Listen."

She began to sing in a sweet voice. The hawks fell silent. All night long she sang to them, and they sat like feathered statues on their perches, listening.

In the morning Albion said, "You are as talented as you are kind and brave. If you had run from them, they would have pecked and clawed you without mercy. What do you want now?"

"I want a ring for my finger," said Petronella.

The enchanter gave her a ring made from a single diamond.

All that day and all night Petronella slept, for she was very tired. But early the next morning, she crept into Prince Ferdinand's room. He was sound asleep, wearing purple pajamas.

"Wake up," whispered Petronella. "I am going to rescue you."

Ferdinand awoke and stared sleepily at her. "What time is it?"

"Never mind that," said Petronella. "Come on!"

"But I'm sleepy," Ferdinand objected. "And it's so pleasant here."

Petronella shook her head. "You're not much of a prince," she said grimly. "But you're the best I can do."

She grabbed him by the wrist and dragged him out of bed. She hauled him down the stairs. His horse and

hers were in a separate stable, and she saddled them quickly. She gave the prince a shove, and he mounted. She jumped on her own horse, seized the prince's reins, and away they went like the wind.

They had not gone far when they heard a tremendous thumping. Petronella looked back. A dark cloud rose behind them, and beneath it she saw the enchanter. He was running with great strides, faster than the horses could go.

"What shall we do?" she cried.

"Don't ask me," said Prince Ferdinand grumpily. "I'm all shaken to bits by this fast riding."

Petronella desperately pulled out the comb. "The old man said this would help me!" she said. And because she didn't know what else to do with it, she threw the comb on the ground. At once a forest rose up. The trees were so thick that no one could get between them.

Away went Petronella and the prince. But the enchanter turned himself into an ax and began to chop. Right and left he chopped, slashing, and the trees fell before him.

Soon he was through the wood, and once again Petronella heard his footsteps thumping behind.

She reined in the horses. She took out the mirror and threw it on the ground. At once a wide lake spread out behind them, gray and glittering.

Off they went again. But the enchanter sprang into the water, turning himself into a salmon as he did so. He swam across the lake and leaped out of the water on to the other bank. Petronella heard him coming — *thump! thump!* — behind them again.

This time she threw down the ring. It didn't turn into anything, but lay shining on the ground.

The enchanter came running up. And as he jumped over the ring, it opened wide and then snapped up around him. It held his arms tight to his body, in a magical grip from which he could not escape.

"Well," said Prince Ferdinand, "that's the end of him."

Petronella looked at him in annoyance. Then she looked at the enchanter, held fast in the ring.

"Bother!" she said. "I can't just leave him here. He'll starve to death."

She got off her horse and went up to him. "If I release you," she said, "will you promise to let the prince go free?"

Albion stared at her in astonishment. "Let him go free?" he said. "What are you talking about? I'm glad to get rid of him."

It was Petronella's turn to look surprised. "I don't understand," she said. "Weren't you holding him prisoner?"

"Certainly not," said Albion. "He came to visit me

69

for a weekend. At the end of it, he said, "It's so pleasant here, do you mind if I stay on for another day or two?' I'm very polite and I said, 'Of course.' He stayed on, and on, and on. I didn't like to be rude to a guest and I couldn't just kick him out. I don't know what I'd have done if you hadn't dragged him away."

"But then—" said Petronella, "but then—why did

you come running after him this way?"

"I wasn't chasing him," said the enchanter. "I was chasing *you*. You are just the girl I've been looking for. You are brave and kind and talented, and beautiful as well."

"Oh," said Petronella. "I see."

"Hmmm," said she. "How do I get this ring off you?"

"Give me a kiss."

She did so. The ring vanished from around Albion and reappeared on Petronella's finger.

"I don't know what my parents will say when I come home with you instead of a prince," she said.

"Let's go and find out, shall we?" said the enchanter cheerfully.

He mounted one horse and Petronella the other. And off they trotted, side by side, leaving Prince Ferdinand of Firebright to walk home as best he could.

PHILBERT THE FEARFUL

S ir Philbert Fitzhugh was not very brave. This wouldn't have mattered had he been a merchant or a mason or a mouse-catcher, but he was a knight. Other knights went riding out to slay dragons or rescue princesses, but Sir Philbert stayed comfortably at home taking care of his health, curled up by the fire with a good book and an apple.

"After all," he said, "I am the only one of me I have, and I have to take care of myself."

Everyone said, "Knights ought to be brave as lions."

"Maybe so," replied Sir Philbert. "But *I* think it's more important to keep your health." And he went back to his reading and his fire and his apple. "An apple a day," he added, "keeps the doctor away."

Nevertheless, the doctor came one day and had dinner, and he poked Sir Philbert in the chest and looked at his tongue and felt his pulse. Then he shook his head.

"You're getting flabby," he said sternly. "Look at yourself! You're pale. You've got the beginnings of a pot-belly. I recommend a long trip and a change of scene."

"But I get homesick," Sir Philbert protested.

The doctor snorted. "Fiddlesticks! Tomorrow morning," said he, "three bold knights are going to search for the emperor's daughter, who has been kidnapped by an enchanter named Brasilgore. I order you to go with them. The adventure will be the best thing for you."

The next morning at half-past four, the three bold knights started out on their quest. With them was a fourth knight, not so bold. It was Sir Philbert.

He had plenty of warm blankets rolled up behind his saddle. He had plenty of food and medicine in his saddlebags. But he was far from happy.

The other three knights, however, were perfectly happy. They were named Sir Hugo of Brandish, Sir Armet of Anguish, and Sir Brian of Thump. Their armor was rusty and dented from many adventures. In their saddlebags they carried nothing but bread and hard cheese. Their mustaches were as fierce as their talk.

"We'll slay Brasilgore the enchanter, and find the emperor's daughter, or die in the attempt!" roared Sir Brian.

"Then I certainly hope we find her," mumbled Sir Philbert.

They traveled for many days until they came to a wide, sad plain. Nothing grew there but twisted thorn bushes and purple heather. A wind from the north blew steadily over it. They rode and rode through the heather and into the wind, and at noon they came to a tower. It was high and black. It had one window at the top and a door in front which was a good deal higher than a house.

As they gazed up at it, wondering what it was for, a maiden put her head out of the window.

"Help, help!" she cried.

Sir Brian shaded his eyes. "Are you a prisoner?" he called.

"Yes, I am. Please go away," said the maiden.

"Eh?" Sir Brian looked puzzled. "But you just said, 'Help, help.'"

"Oh, dear, I know I did. I'm sorry. I said, 'Help, help, but I meant go away.'"

"But why?" asked Sir Hugo of Brandish.

Just then the enormous door opened. "That's why," said the maiden. "Alas, alas, this is the end of you. Good-bye."

Out stepped a giant a good deal higher than a house. He drew a deep breath, stretched, and yawned. It sounded like a thunderstorm overhead.

Sir Hugo lowered his lance. "Stand back, all of you," he shouted. "This giant is mine!"

He rode straight at the giant's ankle and thrust his lance.

"Oh, well done," said Sir Brian.

The giant uttered a yell, "Hornets!" He stamped his foot angrily. Sir Hugo disappeared.

"Adventures!" groaned Sir Philbert. "I just wish that rotten doctor were here."

The other two knights stared uneasily at each other and then at the giant who was grumbling like an earthquake.

Sir Philbert quickly unfastened his big roll of blan-

kets. He shook them out. He turned his horse and began to gallop away, letting the blankets stream behind him like banners.

The giant saw Sir Philbert and made a giant stride to mash him. Sir Philbert let go of the blankets. They blew away in the endless wind. They flew up and plastered themselves over the giant's eyes. He missed his footing, stumbled on a rock, and fell on his head with a crash. Since he was so much bigger and heavier than an ordinary person, he fell with a far bigger and heavier crash. It was the end of him.

Sir Armet and Sir Brian trotted over and stared at the giant's body. They shook their heads.

"Listen," said Sir Armet, "I don't think that was very sporting."

"It was nothing but an accident," Sir Brian agreed. "Philbert didn't kill the giant. He killed himself."

"Yes, I suppose he did," said Sir Philbert. He opened his helmet and mopped his forehead. "But I came on this quest for my health, you know. It wouldn't have been very healthy to go the way poor Hugo went, now would it?"

The maiden came running out of the tower. Sir Philbert took off his helmet, for he was always very polite.

"I'm glad to say you are no longer a prisoner, miss," he said.

"Oh, thank you," smiled the maiden, who had large, merry brown eyes and long brown hair in two braids down her back. "I'll just get my things, if you'll wait a minute."

"What?" huffed Sir Brian. "Get your things?"

"Of course. I'm coming with you. You rescued me, didn't you?"

"You can't come with us," said Sir Armet. "It's much too dangerous."

"Besides, we haven't an extra horse," said Sir Brian.

"She can ride with me," Sir Philbert said.

The maiden smiled at him. She ran into the tower and soon returned with four large bundles. They hung the bundles on Sir Philbert's horse, and Sir Philbert said it was just as well his blankets had all blown away. Then the maiden—whose name was Victoria—got up behind, and away they rode once more.

Victoria said, "I was watching from the window. Did you really expect those blankets to fly up over the giant's face?"

Sir Philbert sighed. "I hoped so," he said.

"If they hadn't, what would you have done?"

"I would have kept on riding as fast as I could. I didn't see how else I could beat a giant that tall."

"But shouldn't a knight be brave?"

"Oh, yes," said Sir Philbert. "But on the other hand, I'm the only one of me I have, and I have to take care of myself."

Victoria nodded. "That's reasonable," she said.

They rode on. At last they came to a high place. The road ran over a peak that sparkled with glassy ice. On each side, the rock fell away in steep cliffs, down, down, to glittering rock below. Sir Brian's horse suddenly reared and skittered around. Sir Armet's horse reared too. After a bit Sir Philbert and Victoria caught up with them and saw what they saw. Their horse couldn't rear because it was too heavily loaded.

There was a cockatrice in the way. It had the body of a serpent and the head and legs of a rooster. Its scales were green and shiny in the icy light. Its long serpent

tongue flicked in and out of its cock's beak, and its round, evil eyes rolled forward to look at them. It strutted as tall as a man.

"Hmm," said Sir Philbert. "It might be better to go back and find another way. After all, we have a lady with us."

"Pah! You are a coward, sir," said Sir Armet. "Stand back, all of you."

He lowered his lance and galloped forward.

"Oh, dear," Sir Philbert whispered to Victoria.

Sir Armet's lance shattered on the green scales. The cockatrice hissed. It darted its rooster's beak forward on its snaky neck. Sir Armet's horse gave a scream and plunged over the edge of the cliff with Sir Armet.

"Stand back, all of you," said Sir Brian nervously. He began to lower his lance. But Sir Philbert caught his elbow.

"Wait a minute," said Sir Philbert. "I just thought of something I'd like to try."

He got off his horse. "Victoria, my dear," he said, "have you a mirror?"

"Oh, yes," she answered. She opened one of her bundles and took out a large, golden looking glass with her initial "V" in emeralds on the back.

Sir Philbert took it and walked forward, his armor squeaking and clinking in the still, cold air. The cockatrice shot out its fearsome head once again. Sir Philbert held out the mirror.

The cockatrice stared into it. Then it gave a dithering hiss of horror, spread its wings, and flew away over the peaks.

Sir Philbert returned the looking glass to Victoria. He was shaking like a leaf.

"Why, how brave of you!" cried Victoria, giving him a hug.

"No, not very brave," said Sir Philbert. "The only thing a cockatrice is afraid of is another cockatrice. I was pretty sure it would fly off when it saw its face in the mirror. I read that in a book," he added humbly.

"Then it was very clever of you," Victoria said firmly.

"Humph!" grunted Sir Brian. "Clever? I'm not so sure a knight *ought* to be clever."

Sir Philbert hung his head. "I know. But you see, I'm the only one of me I have...."

"Suppose we have a bite of lunch and then push on," Sir Brian said briskly.

When they had finished eating, they followed the road over the top of the mountain and down the other side. After a time, Sir Philbert remarked, "These trees are growing in rows, almost like a park."

"Rubbish!" said Sir Brian. "It's a wild wood."

"There's no underbrush either," Sir Philbert continued.

"Ridiculous!" said Sir Brian. "Next you'll be telling me you see a castle."

"I see a castle," Sir Philbert said.

Sure enough, the trees ended at a bridge, and on the other side of it there was a gloomy castle with many turrets.

"Ha!" Sir Brian exclaimed. "The castle of the enchanter!"

"Are you sure?" asked Sir Philbert.

"Of course I'm sure. Don't you think I know what an enchanter's castle looks like?" Sir Brian retorted.

They rode across the bridge and under a gateway like a giant's yawn, into a paved courtyard. All was silent.

Sir Brian rubbed his hands together. "Now then," he said, "The enchanter is probably upstairs in his den. I'll go after him. If anything happens to me — which isn't very likely because I know how to handle these fellows — just remember one rule. You must hold on to the enchanter until he surrenders. He will turn himself into all sorts of beasts: a lion, a wolf, a dragon, anything. As long as you hold him you're safe.

If you let go of him, he'll magic you, and — *poof!*"

Sir Philbert nodded. "I've read all about that in—" he began, but Sir Brian was gone.

Sir Philbert rubbed his chin. "You know," he said to Victoria, "I'm not at all sure this is the right castle."

"Never mind," said Victoria.

"But I *do* mind. I think I'd better follow Brian. Suppose something happens to him?"

"Suppose something happens to you?" said Victoria.

"Don't let's talk about it," Sir Philbert gulped.

He walked into the castle. There was a large cobwebby hall with a winding, dusty stair at one end of it. He could see Sir Brian's footprints in the dust. He began to follow them.

Now Sir Brian had climbed the stairs, and he had found, at the top, a heavy door opening into a tower room. Inside, there was a little old man with a bristle of untidy hair. Sir Brian sprang in and seized him by the neck.

"Ha, foul wizard," shouted Sir Brian, "I have thee!"

The old man at once turned into a lion. Sir Brian held fast. The lion became a fanged wolf. Sir Brian with a laugh still held him. The wolf became a dragon. Sir Brian held on. The dragon, in the blink of an eye, turned into a lady.

"Oh, you're hurting me," said the lady. "Not very knightly of you."

"I beg your pardon," said Sir Brian. He let go at once. The enchanter promptly waved his hand and turned Sir Brian into a pelican, which gave a dismal squawk and flew out the window.

The enchanter changed back into himself and began to dust off his cloak. At that instant, Sir Philbert, who

had seen the whole thing from the doorway, rushed in and grabbed the enchanter by the neck.

"What? Another one?" shrieked the enchanter.

He was so confused that he turned himself into a dreadful combination of lion, wolf, dragon, and woman all at once. Sir Philbert gritted his teeth and hung on. The enchanter than turned into a unicorn, a falcon, a salmon, a chest of drawers, a saber-toothed tiger, and a burning wastepaper basket. Sir Philbert held on for dear life. At last, the enchanter turned into a wasp. This time, Sir Philbert almost did let go. But he thought of his health and of Victoria and of poor blustering Sir Brian, who was now a pelican, and he gripped the wasp tightly. It didn't sting him after all. Instead, it turned back into the enchanter, looking extremely sulky.

"Very well," he panted. "You've won. What is your wish?"

"I want you to take the spell off Sir Brian," said Sir Philbert.

"What, right now?"

"At once."

The enchanter chuckled disagreeably. "Very well," he said. He waved his hand. Sir Brian, who was at that moment flying low over a swamp, changed back into himself and fell plop! into the mud.

"Anything else?" said the enchanter.

"Yes," said Sir Philbert, remembering the reason for the quest. "I want you to let the emperor's daughter go."

"Let her go? How can I let her go when I haven't got her?"

"Oh, my," groaned Sir Philbert. "I knew it was the wrong castle. Well, who did kidnap her?"

"She was kidnapped by Brasilgore," said the enchanter. "And she has already been rescued."

"She has? Where is she?"

"Downstairs in my courtyard," snarled the enchanter. "Now, if there's nothing else I can do for you, will you please go away?"

But Sir Philbert had already gone, down the stairs two at a time.

"And so Brasilgore the enchanter was a giant," he

said as he and Victoria went trotting off together, she riding more comfortably on Sir Brian's horse. "But why didn't you tell us?"

"You never asked me," Victoria replied.

"That's true. Well, I suppose I'd better take you home to your father as quickly as possible."

They traveled until they came to the emperor's empire. They entered the great city, and all the people ran out to cheer and stare and point. They came to the castle, and there was the emperor on a throne of ivory and emeralds. There also was Sir Brian, looking very muddy and rusty and bothered.

"Victoria, my darling, I'm so glad to see you again," said the emperor, embracing her. "Sir Brian was telling me how he had failed to find you."

Victoria hugged her father. "I must just tell you everything that has happened," she cried. And so she did.

When she was finished, the emperor said, "I have sworn to give half my kingdom and my daughter's hand to the man brave enough to rescue her."

Sir Philbert blushed. "My lord," he said, "I really don't want half your kingdom. I have a nice little castle of my own, and it's all I can do to manage it — but I *would* rather like to have Victoria."

Victoria smiled and took his hand.

Then Sir Brian interrupted. "My lord emperor," he cried, "that man didn't rescue your daughter by bravery. He killed the giant by accident and the cockatrice by a trick."

"Dear me," said the emperor. He stroked his beard thoughtfully. "Now let me get this straight. Where is Sir Hugo of Brandish?"

"He died a hero's death, sire," said Sir Brian.

"I see. And Sir Armet of Anguish?"

"Perished bravely in combat."

"Ah. And as for you, you'd still be a pelican if it hadn't been for Sir Philbert, eh?"

Sir Brian frowned. "But he is a coward!" he said.

"Ah, yes, there's that." The emperor turned to one of his servants and whispered in his ear. The servant turned pale and ran off. He came back in a few moments with a large box. From the box came a loud and angry humming.

"Now, gallant sirs," said the emperor, "here is a box containing a wasp's nest. I'd like one of you to reach inside and catch a wasp for me. There is no reward. I just want a wasp."

Sir Brian reached out a hand, listened to the furious humming, winced, and drew it back. Nobody else moved.

"You see," said the emperor. "When Sir Philbert held on to the enchanter he was being quite as brave as was necessary. Sir Philbert, will you reach in and get me a wasp?"

Sir Philbert swallowed hard. He had had more prac-

87

tice than anyone, so to speak, but he didn't much want to do it again. Then, suddenly, he had an idea. He grinned. He pulled on one of his iron gloves, reached into the box, and took out a wasp.

Victoria laughed. She said to her father, "He's the only one of him there is, and I'm the only one of me there is, and he knows how to take care of both of us."

"Quite right," said the emperor. "I'd much rather have my daughter married to someone with sense enough to stay alive and take care of her than have her married to a pelican."

So Philbert and Victoria were married and rode happily home to take care of each other.